DIDN'T
Didn't Do It

By **Bradford Morrow**

Illustrated by **Gahan Wilson**

G. P. Putnam's Sons

G. P. PUTNAM'S SONS
A division of Penguin Young Readers Group.
Published by The Penguin Group.
Penguin Group (USA) Inc., 375 Hudson Street, New York, NY 10014, U.S.A.
Penguin Group (Canada), 90 Eglinton Avenue East, Suite 700, Toronto, Ontario, Canada M4P 2Y3
(a division of Pearson Penguin Canada Inc.).
Penguin Books Ltd, 80 Strand, London WC2R 0RL, England.
Penguin Ireland, 25 St. Stephen's Green, Dublin 2, Ireland (a division of Penguin Books Ltd.).
Penguin Group (Australia), 250 Camberwell Road, Camberwell, Victoria 3124, Australia
(a division of Pearson Australia Group Pty Ltd).
Penguin Books India Pvt Ltd, 11 Community Centre, Panchsheel Park, New Delhi - 110 017, India.
Penguin Group (NZ), Cnr Airborne and Rosedale Roads, Albany, Auckland 1310, New Zealand
(a division of Pearson New Zealand Ltd).
Penguin Books (South Africa) (Pty) Ltd, 24 Sturdee Avenue, Rosebank, Johannesburg 2196, South Africa.
Penguin Books Ltd, Registered Offces: 80 Strand, London WC2R 0RL, England.

Design by Katrina Damkoehler. Text set in Clichee. The art was done in pen and ink, with watercolor.

Library of Congress Cataloging-in-Publication Data
Morrow, Bradford.
Didn't didn't do it / by Bradford Morrow ; Illustrated by Gahan Wilson.   p. cm.
Summary: Several children start to build a tree house but change their minds when
they come across a family of birds that already lives in the tree.
[1. Birds—Fiction. 2. Tree houses—Fiction.]
I. Title: Did not did not do it. II. Wilson, Gahan, ill. III. Title.
PZ7.M84539Did 2007   [E]—dc22   2005032659

ISBN 978-0-399-24480-3
10 9 8 7 6 5 4 3 2 1
First Impression

Neither did **DOESN'T**.

DOESN'T didn't do it

because **DIDN'T** wouldn't.

WOULDN'T
couldn't

because **SHOULDN'T** can't.

And **CAN'T** didn't do it

since **DIDN'T** doesn't.

DOESN'T didn't do what SHOULDN'T couldn't,

what
DOESN'T
wouldn't.

WOULDN'T
didn't do it

since **DIDN'T** didn't,

and
DOESN'T doesn't

and
SHOULDN'T
shouldn't

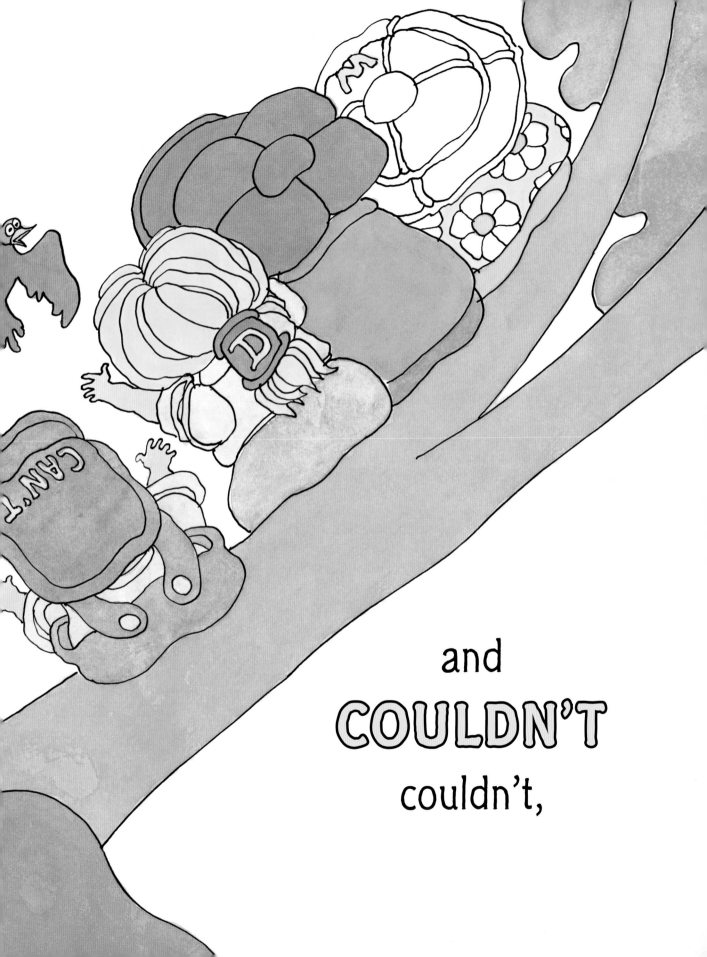

and
COULDN'T
couldn't,

so it never got done!